Brian the Giant

Written by Vivian French
Illustrated by Sue Heap

WALKER BOOKS
AND SUBSIDIARIES
LONDON · BOSTON · SYDNEY · AUCKLAND

Brian the Giant lived in a house on the top of a hill. It was a giant house with a giant kitchen and giant jugs and jars. Because Brian LOVED eating — especially muffins.

milk

pg 24 cakes!

Brian's Recipes

5

Muffin recipe

*

1. Measure these ingredients
   into a bowl:

   2 cups flour
   1/2 cup sugar (white or brown)
   1/2 teaspoon salt
   4 teaspoons baking powder

   and mix them together.

Multiply everything by 100 for GIANTS

2. Measure these ingredients
   into a different bowl:
   1 beaten egg
   1/4 cup corn oil
   1 cup milk
   and mix them together.

3. Pour the milk mixture into the
   flour mixture and mix them together.

4. Add one cup of blueberries and mix
   in gently.

5. Spoon mixture into 10 paper muffin
   cases and bake in a preheated oven
   at 200°C/400°F/gas mark 6 for 15–20
   minutes. Take out when brown and
   smelling yummy.

Most FAVOURITE muffins 10/10

But Brian was NOT good at cooking.

Brian moaned and groaned as he measured and mixed his muffins.

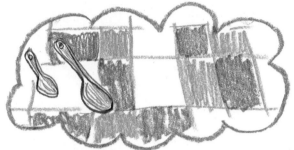

Is it teaspoons or tablespoons?

Is that sugar or salt?

How much is a cupful? A teacup, an egg cup, a coffee cup?

Sometimes Brian's muffins were hard.

Sometimes Brian's muffins didn't rise.

Sometimes Brian's muffins were burnt.

But on Monday Brian's muffins were
PERFECT, and he was very, very happy.

Brian put his muffins on a plate and made a big pot of tea. He sat at the table to eat his muffins, and dropped crumbs all over the floor.

"YUM!" Brian said as he finished his last mouthful. "What wonderful muffins!"
"They are indeed!" said the mouse who lived under the clock.
"Would you mind if I ate the crumbs?"
"Please do," said Brian.

YUM!

On Tuesday Brian made ten perfect blueberry muffins. "Hurrah!" he said. "I shall ask Aunt Pansy to tea."

Brian put his muffins on a plate.
He put the plate in his larder.
Then he marched over to Aunt
Pansy's house.

"Come to tea, Aunt Pansy," Brian said. "I've made ten perfect blueberry muffins."
But Aunt Pansy was busy.

Brian marched back to his house.

He put the kettle on for tea.
He opened his larder and
took out the plate.
Brian stared.
The plate was …

Brian scratched his head.
Then he had an idea.
"Mouse! Have you been
eating my muffins?"

The mouse popped out from
under the clock.

"Me, Mr Brian?" she asked. "How
could one teeny mouse eat ten
great big blueberry muffins?"
Brian thought about it.

"No," he said. "You're much
too small."

On Wednesday Brian's muffins were as hard as nails.

On Thursday Brian's muffins were as flat as a pancake.

On Friday Brian burnt his muffins to a cinder.

On Saturday Brian cooked ten
perfect chocolate muffins.
"Hurrah!" he said, and put his muffins
on a plate.
He put the plate in his larder.

At four o'clock Brian
put the kettle on.
He laid the table.
He opened his larder
and took out the plate.

Brian stared.

The plate was …

The mouse popped out
from under the clock.
"Me, Mr Brian?" she asked.
"How could one teeny
mouse eat ten great
big chocolate muffins?"
Brian thought about it.
"No," he said. "You're
much too small."

KNOCK KNOCK!!

Brian hurried to
open the door.
"Oh, Aunt Pansy!"
he cried. "Somebody's
eaten my muffins
AGAIN!"

Oh,
Aunt Pansy!

Aunt Pansy looked at
the empty plate.
She looked at the mouse
twirling her whiskers.
"I've got a VERY special
recipe for muffins," she said.

Aunt Pansy measured
and Brian mixed.

They put their muffins in the oven.
"They'll be ready in fifteen minutes," Aunt Pansy said.

Aunt Pansy and Brian played snap.

Aunt Pansy won.

Then their muffins were ready.

"PERFECT!" said Brian. "Shall we eat
them?"

"No," Aunt Pansy said. "Just put them
in your larder."

Brian walked with Aunt Pansy
to his gate.
"Goodbye, Brian," she said. "Now
hurry back inside!"

As Brian opened his front door he heard a noise.

ATCHOO!!

ATCHOO!!

ATCHOO!!

He hurried inside.
There was one little
mouse on the table.

There were two little mice
on the cushion.

There were three little mice
on the shelf.

There were four little mice
on the floor.

There were mice all over Brian's house … and they all had crumbs on their whiskers.

Brian looked in his larder.

His muffins were gone.

"YOU ATE MY MUFFINS!" he roared.

"ATCHOO!" said the biggest mouse.

"I told my sister about your muffins …"

"And I told my friends …"

ATCHOO!!

"And we told our brothers …"

ATCHOO!!

"And we told our cousins …"

ATCHOO!!

The littlest mouse hopped across
the table.
"But nobody said you made
muffins with PEPPER!" he said.

Brian sat down on his chair.

"Well, well, well," he said.

The biggest mouse held out

a teeny plate.

"Before we go, may we offer

you a muffin?" she said.

Brian peered at it.
"Can YOU make muffins?"
he asked.
"Of course," said the mouse.
"Making muffins is what we
like doing best."

Brian scratched his chin.
"Could you help me make
perfect muffins?"
The mouse nodded.

Of course!

"Then," said Brian,
"I think you ought
to stay."

So the mice helped Brian
to measure and mix.
And from then on his
muffins were ALWAYS
perfect …

... except when he muddled the sugar and salt!

For my friend Joel, with love xx
V.F.

For Davey
S.H.

First published 2005 by Walker Books Ltd
87 Vauxhall Walk, London SE11 5HJ

2 4 6 8 10 9 7 5 3

Text © 2005 Vivian French
Illustrations © 2005 Sue Heap

The right of Vivian French and Sue Heap to be identified
as author and illustrator respectively of this work has
been asserted by them in accordance with the
Copyright, Designs and Patents Act 1988

This book has been typeset in Gill Sans MT Schoolbook

Handlettering by Sue Heap

Printed in China

British Library Cataloguing in Publication Data:
a catalogue record for this book
is available from the British Library

ISBN 978-1-84428-963-9

www.walkerbooks.co.uk